kitten
red yellow blue

Peter Catalanotto

A Richard Jackson Book • Atheneum Books for Young Readers
New York   London   Toronto   Sydney

Mrs. Tuttle's cat, Sophia,
had 16 calico kittens.

Everybody in the neighborhood
wanted one.

Sophia wonders how Mrs. Tuttle tells
the kittens apart.

Mrs. Tuttle finds it quite simple.

Red kitten rescues with Dave, the firefighter.

Yellow kitten digs
with Tom, the construction worker.

Blue kitten patrols with Francine, the police officer.

NO FISHING
NO DOGS
NO SMOKING
NO BICYCLES
NO RADIOS

Green kitten gardens
with Paul, the landscaper.

Purple kitten performs with Zack, the musician.

Orange kitten plays
with Chelsea,
the basketball player.

Brown kitten delivers with Katie, the courier.

Black kitten exercises
with Peri, the karate teacher.

White kitten cooks
with Mario, the chef.

[Gray] kitten works with Benny, the mechanic.

Pink kitten practices with Zoe, the ballerina.

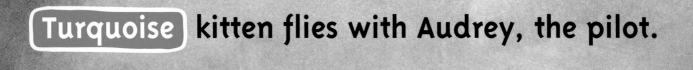 kitten flies with Audrey, the pilot.

Rust kitten repairs with Tony, the plumber.

Teal kitten cures
with Louann,
the pediatrician.

Tan kitten bags
with Doug, the clerk.

Chartreuse kitten directs
with Celia, the crossing guard.

Sophia misses
her babies
very much . . .

. . . so Mrs. Tuttle has a party.

To Dr. Lynn Orlando, for her kindness

Atheneum Books for Young Readers • An imprint of Simon & Schuster Children's Publishing Division • 1230 Avenue of the Americas, New York, New York 10020
Copyright © 2005 by Peter Catalanotto • All rights reserved, including the right of reproduction in whole or in part in any form. • Book design by Abelardo
Martínez • The text for this book is set in Triplex Bold. • The illustrations for this book are rendered in watercolor. • Manufactured in China • First Edition
10 9 8 7 6 5 4 3 2 1 • Library of Congress Cataloging-in-Publication Data • Catalanotto, Peter. • Kitten red, yellow, blue / Peter Catalanotto.— 1st ed. • p. cm.
"A Richard Jackson book." • Summary: After placing the red kitten with Dave, the firefighter, and the blue kitten with Francine, the police officer, Mrs.
Tuttle finds homes for fourteen other colorful kittens. • ISBN 0-689-86562-7 • [1. Color—Fiction. 2. Occupations—Fiction. 3. Cats—Fiction. 4. Animals—
Infancy—Fiction.] I. Title. • PZ7.C26878Ki 2005 • [E]—dc22 • 2003019584